D0570510

# Daisy
## the
# Doctor

### Felicity Brooks

### Illustrated by Jo Litchfield

### Designed by Nickey Butler

Medical consultants: Kristina Routh MBChB,
Andrew Jordan MBChB MRCGP
Americanization editor: Carrie Armstrong

This is Daisy the Doctor,
taking her son Ben to school.
After she's dropped him off,
she drives to work.

The traffic can be terrible.

Daisy works at the Medical Center. Her job is to help people stay healthy and to treat them when they are sick.

These are the people Daisy works with:

Alice the Receptionist

Michael the Nurse

Doctor Ashwin Kapoor

3

The waiting room is already packed with people when Daisy arrives.

Dr. Daisy Flowers

Alice hands Daisy a pile of notes about her patients.

Children can play with toys while they wait to see the doctor. Grown-ups usually prefer to read magazines.

4

"Good morning," says Alice cheerfully.
"You have lots of patients to see today."

In her office, Daisy checks her computer to see who has appointments.

Daisy's computer is linked to Alice's, so she always knows who's coming to see her.

| Patient | Status | | | |
|---|---|---|---|---|
| Isaac Sanchez | waiting | | | 35 Acacia Ave |
| Aruna Gupta | waiting | | | 64 Randolph Ave |
| Jon Potman | waiting | | | 134 Long Lane |
| Kirsteen Carter | cancelled | | | 275 Station Rd |
| Zoe Khan | | | | 81 Market Drive |
| Cameron Tate | | | | 42 Park St |
| Joey Marshall | | | | 124 Main St |
| Rani Iheeta | | | | 3 Longwall St |
| Megan Williams | | | | 31 Long Lane |
| Peter O'Grady | | | | 84 Denver Drive |
| Ali Milailo | | | | |
| Carrie Pearce | | | | |
| Francesca Lopez | | | | |
| Kate Parker | | | | |
| Ruth Levy | | | | |

May 1 2 3 4 5 6
7 8 9 10 11 12 13
14 15 16 17 18 19 20
21 22 23 24 25 26 27
28 29 30 31

Auntie P's birthday - flowers?

Ben swimming tomorrow

Pears
Figs
Toothpaste
Eggs

At nine o'clock exactly, Daisy calls her first patient into her examining room. Do you know his name?

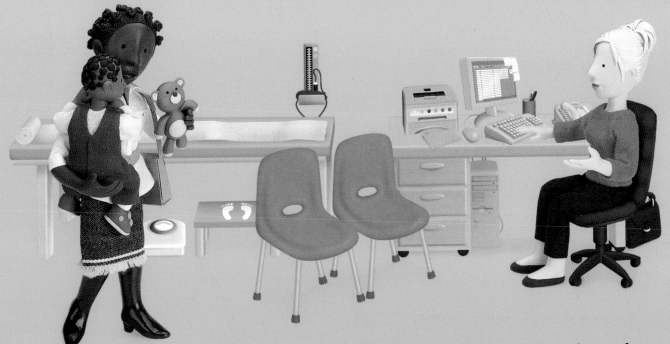

He's a little boy named Isaac Sanchez.

"How can I help?" Daisy asks.
"Poor little Isaac's been up all night with an awful earache," says his mom.

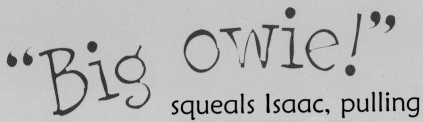

"Big owie!" squeals Isaac, pulling on his sore ear.

Daisy gets out her otoscope to check Isaac's ears. He looks a little worried, so Daisy shows him how to use it on his teddy bear. "See, it doesn't hurt your bear," she says.

Then she looks inside Isaac's ears.

"Hmmm... his left ear's very red," she says. "He has an infection, so he'll need some antibiotics and painkillers."

Amoxicillin 125mg/
1x5ml spoon
3 times a day

Dr. Daisy Flowers

The Medical Center
Wellbrook Green
Littletown

Daisy prints out
a prescription
and signs it.

"Please come back and see me in a day or two
if he's not better," she says as she hands the
prescription to Isaac's mom.

Next, in comes a mom with Aruna, a tiny baby, and a small boy named Ravi.
"We're here for Aruna's check-up," says the mom.

Daisy examines Aruna carefully.

She weighs baby Aruna and asks her mom about how she's feeding and sleeping.

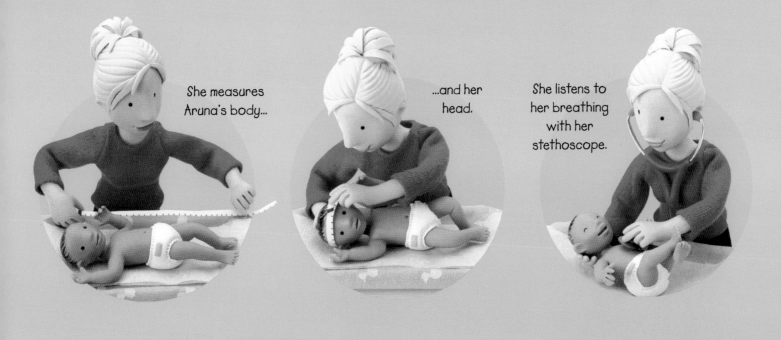

She measures Aruna's body...

...and her head.

She listens to her breathing with her stethoscope.

"Aruna's doing fine," Daisy tells the mom.

Just then, Alice knocks and opens the door from Reception.

"Someone's had an accident!" she says. "Can you see him?"

Outside in the waiting room Daisy can hear crying.

A young boy is holding his arm and wailing.

Dr. Daisy F

"His... his arm won't stop bleeding,"
says his mom, out of breath.
"Come right in," says Daisy.

13

"What's your name, young man?" asks Daisy as she leads them into her room.

"A-a-a-lex," sobs the boy.

Daisy comforts Alex and gently examines his arm. "It's a nasty cut," she says, "but you don't need to go to the hospital. Michael the Nurse can treat it here."

"Can you tell me what happened?" she asks.

"I was on... on the yellow swing in the playground," sobs Alex,

"and I tried to jump off, like I always do..."

"...but someone had left a bike there and I... I landed on it – BANG! And it really, really hurt."

Ooww!

Alex stops crying. He has to be brave when Michael the Nurse treats the cut.

First Michael cleans the cut with antiseptic and dries it carefully.

Next, he puts little sticky strips across it to help it heal.

Then he puts a dressing on it to keep it clean.

"Try to keep it dry," says Michael, adding a bandage. "And your mom'll need to change the dressing every day."

"But I can still do the play, can't I?" Alex asks anxiously.

"Alex is a pirate in his school play tonight," explains his mom.

"Oh, I think you'll make a wonderful wounded pirate," laughs Michael.

Now Daisy the Doctor is running late
and still has a lot more patients to see:

a shy young boy
with tummyache;

a big bald baby
with a cough;

an itchy little
girl with eczema
on her knee;

a boy with
spots on his
tummy;

a wheezy girl
who has asthma;

a tall teenager with
a sprained ankle;

a small girl
with a rash...

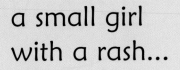

...and that's not all. Daisy jots down a few notes about each patient.

Francesca Lopez - expecting twins

Kate Parker - sprained wrist ☆

Ali Milailo - man with pains in chest

Ruth Levy - aching joints

Isabelle Breux - very bad headache

Lee Chang -

Randall Bla

Mairi Mc

These are some pages of Daisy's notebook. (She did the doodles too.)

When she's seen all of them, at last it's time to go home.

"I'm exhausted," says Daisy to Alice. "I haven't had time for lunch, and I've got a headache."

"Maybe you should see a doctor!" says Alice.

"Goodbye!"

Photography: MMStudios

With thanks to Staedtler UK for providing
the Fimo® material for models,
and to Moir Medical Centre, Nottingham, UK

www.usborne.com
First published in 2004 by Usborne Publishing Ltd.,
Usborne House, 83-85 Saffron Hill, London EC1N 8RT, England. Copyright ©2004 Usborne Publishing Ltd.

The name Usborne and the devices 🎈 🌐 are Trade Marks of Usborne Publishing Ltd. All rights reserved. No part
of this publication may be reproduced, stored in a retrieval system, or transmitted in any form or by any means,
electronic, mechanical, photocopying, recording or otherwise without the prior permission of the publisher. A.E.
First published in America 2005.
Printed in Dubai.